PUTTY ATTACK!

By Francine Hughes

A PARACHUTE PRESS BOOK

GROSSET & DUNLAP • NEW YORK

A PARACHUTE PRESS BOOK
Parachute Press, Inc.
156 Fifth Avenue
New York, NY 10010

Published by Grosset & Dunlap, Inc., a member of The Putnam &
Grosset Group, New York. GROSSET & DUNLAP is a trademark of
Grosset & Dunlap, Inc. Published simultaneously in Canada.

Creative Consultant: Cheryl Saban.

With special thanks to Cheryl Saban, Debi Young, Ban Pryor, and
Sherry Stack.

Printed in the U.S.A.
August 1994
Library of Congress Catalog Card Number: 94-77643
ISBN: 0-448-40930-5
A B C D E F G H I J

PROLOGUE

Evil forces beware. Five ordinary teenagers are about to morph into—the Mighty Morphin Power Rangers.

Their incredible powers come from Zordon, a good wizard trapped in another dimension. Zordon has given each teenager a

magic coin—a Power Morpher—
and super strength drawn from
the spirits of the dinosaurs.

When things get really tough,
the Power Rangers call upon their
Dinozords—giant robots they
drive into battle.

Power Rangers, dinosaur spirits, and amazing robots—together
these incredible forces protect
the Earth.

So—get ready. *It's morphin
time!*

CHAPTER 1

The Halls were buzzing at Angel Grove High School on Friday afternoon. Everybody was excited about the weekend.

"I can't wait to go scuba diving," Trini said to Jason and Zack, two of her best friends. She flipped her long, straight black hair over one shoulder, then closed her locker.

Jason flashed her an easygoing smile as he zipped up his red sweatshirt. "When I show you the reef I found, you won't believe it. It's awesome!"

"I bet we'll see some really big fish," Zack said, his dark eyes sparkling with excitement.

Just then Bulk, the school bully, pushed his way through the crowd. His pal Skull trailed behind him.

"Well, if *big* is what you're looking for, you won't have to look far," Trini said, pointing to Bulk.

Lots of things were big about Bulk. He was one of the biggest kids in school. With his scraggly ponytail and his beat-up old leather jacket, he was the biggest mess, too. And he was definitely the biggest troublemaker.

Skinny, dim-witted Skull had on his usual outfit—black on black on black. The head of a fish stuck out of the front of his black cap, and a fish tail poked out the back.

"Don't count on seeing any big fish, dweebs," Bulk told the three friends. "They'll all be at the end of *my* hook!"

Bulk opened his locker. It was jammed with junk. It suited messy Bulk perfectly.

He stuck a hefty arm inside and yanked out a fish net. *Crash!*

Fishing rods came tumbling out. *Bang!* Hooks and bait boxes and fishing gear clattered to the ground. Smelly boots filled with stale water fell to the floor with a sloshing, squishy noise.

Trini jumped back so that the water wouldn't splash her. Zack and Jason held their noses.

Clumsily, Skull scurried to gather the gear. Nets, worms, boots, and fishing poles.

"Hey," Skull said, tugging on a line. "I got a bite!"

Skull yanked the rod, and Bulk jerked forward. The line had snagged Bulk's belt loop.

Skull pulled harder on the line, unaware that he was reeling in

Bulk. "It's a big one. I hope it doesn't break the line!"

"Fish-brain!" Bulk shouted as Skull's hook pulled Bulk's pants down.

Trini giggled at Bulk's rainbow-colored underwear.

Bulk turned bright red. He tried to tug his pants back up, but he got tangled up in the fishing line. Yelling and jerking and hopelessly snarled, Bulk and Skull tripped down the hall.

"I don't think the fish need to worry about those two," Zack joked. He plopped a baseball cap on his curly dark hair and smiled.

Just then Kimberly and Billy joined their friends. The five best friends looked like ordinary teenagers. And everybody thought they were just that. But everybody was wrong. The five friends shared the world's biggest secret: Each one of them had incredible superpowers. When evil forces threatened the Earth, they used their amazing powers and changed into the Mighty Morphin Power Rangers!

But right now, the only thing on their minds was to enjoy the upcoming weekend.

"Hey, Billy," Jason said, "why don't you come to the beach with us? We're going scuba diving. I'm a certified diving instructor, you know."

Billy looked uncomfortable as he pushed up his glasses. He shifted his books from one arm to the other, then pretended to polish the snaps of his overalls. Finally, he spoke. "My apologies, Jason. But I have a regrettable dislike for fish."

"Kimberly, how about you?" Trini asked her friend.

Kimberly smoothed her pretty pink sweater. Then she checked her light brown hair in her locker mirror. "Nope, Billy and I are going on a picnic in the park."

Billy nodded eagerly. "It'll be nice. We'll be right by the park lake." But suddenly a shadow crossed Billy's face. *A lake?* That meant water…and maybe…fish!

"Of course we'll stay a carefully planned distance from the lake and any fishy unpleasantries," he added quickly.

Far away in her fortress on the moon, the evil Rita Repulsa spied on the teens through her magic telescope. She was a terrifying sight. Her dark eyes narrowed into scary slits. Her bony hands with their long, pointy black nails held the telescope in a tight grip.

She nudged Goldar, her chief warrior—hard—with her bony elbow. "Wake up, you moron," she screeched.

Goldar jumped to attention, his

red eyes glowing. "At your command, O Evil Empress."

Rita had a mission—a plan to take over the Earth. And long ago, she had vowed not to let anyone get in her way. *Especially* not five teenagers from Angel Grove.

As Rita watched Billy through her magic telescope, she was thrilled with what she saw.

"So Billy doesn't like fish, eh?" she remarked to Goldar. The warrior's nasty eyes glowed even brighter.

"Thanks, Billy," Rita cackled happily. "You've just given me an idea. A wonderful, evil idea to finally destroy the Earth!"

CHAPTER 2

At the beach the next day, sunlight danced across the calm ocean water.

"It's a perfect day for scuba diving," Jason said as he checked Trini and Zack's oxygen tanks one last time. He wanted to make sure they were working right.

"Now remember the safety signals," Jason instructed as he zipped up his wet suit. "And stay together!"

Zack hip-hopped in his flippers down to the shore. "Come on, let's go!" he shouted.

"You're on," said Trini, joining him at the shoreline. She was wearing a wet suit exactly like Jason and Zack's.

The three friends put on their face masks and waded into the water.

At the park, Billy and Kimberly spread out a blanket on a large rock near the lake. A warm breeze ruffled Kimberly's hair as she set the picnic basket down.

"What's for lunch?" Billy asked.

"Fish and chips. Is that okay?"

Billy suddenly looked a little sick. "I'll take the chips. But please hold the fish."

"What's with you and fish, anyway?" Kimberly asked, concerned.

"I've had some rather bad fish experiences, Kim. It all started when I was a toddler," he began to explain. "I wanted to recreate a whirlpool effect that I had seen on a TV show, so I put my finger into the lake water and swirled it in circles. It proved to be an exciting lure for one of the hungry fish below. And the fish actually bit me!" Billy finished his story, looking very upset.

Kimberly burst out laughing.

"It's not funny," Billy said. "And once a crab bit me, too! It was awful."

"Well, this fish sandwich won't bite." Kimberly held it out to him.

Billy reluctantly took the sandwich. But he kept it at arm's length. "I don't know…" he said.

Suddenly, a scream pierced the air. "What was that?" Billy asked, scrambling to his feet.

He and Kimberly raced toward the cries at the other end of the lake.

"Oh, no," Kimberly moaned when she saw the source of the screams. "Not Bulk and Skull!"

The two goons shouted with excitement as Bulk struggled with his fishing rod. "I got the big one!" Bulk screamed. "Here it comes!" He yanked hard—and a huge No Fishing sign burst out of the water.

"All right, Bulk!" Skull yelled. "Way to go!"

But Bulk wanted a fish, not a sign. "Clam up!" he shouted at Skull. He angrily tossed the sign on top of a pile of old boots, tires, and garbage—his catch of the day so far.

Suddenly Bulk shouted, "I got one! I got one!"

"Me, too!" Skull cried. "Me, too!"

But once again, Skull's line had caught Bulk's belt loop. And Bulk's line had snagged Skull's. They both gave a giant tug—and sent each other flying into the lake.

Billy and Kimberly burst out laughing. Bulk glared up at them, then snarled at Skull. "That does it, tuna-breath." He stood up and shook the water from his hair. "You scared off all the fish!"

Billy and Kimberly chuckled as they walked away.

"Hey," said Kimberly. "Let's surprise the others down at the beach."

Billy kicked a pebble. "I'm not really into oceans. They're full of fish, you know."

"But they're in the ocean, not on the shore," Kimberly pleaded.

"You have a point," Billy said. "But I'm not going into the water."

"Deal!" Kimberly agreed.

"They're going to the beach?" Rita screeched from the balcony of her fortress on the moon. "They can't go to the beach yet! My new monster isn't ready to meet them. I want my monster!"

She and Goldar stormed into Finster's smelly lab, where the monster-maker was hunched over his latest evil creation. "Where's my monster?" Rita shouted.

"O Supreme Evilness," Finster

said, looking fearfully at the evil queen, "I'm just adding the deadly goo so that the monster will poison the ocean and destroy all of the sea life."

Rita's lips curled into a nasty grin at the thought. But her smile faded quickly.

"Those power brats better not spoil my plans," she shrieked.

"Indeed, Your Badness," Goldar said. "The Putty Patrol can keep them busy."

"Yes!" cried Rita. "Send the Putties!"

With that, Rita's army of mindless clay creatures somersaulted onto the Earth to attack Kimberly and Billy.

CHAPTER 3

"Oh, no," Kimberly shouted as six Putty Patrollers crashed onto their picnic blanket.

Kimberly and Billy saw at once that they were outnumbered. They needed help. "Jason! Trini! Zack!" Kimberly called into the communicator that she wore on her wrist. "We need you!"

No one answered.

"They must still be underwater," Billy said as he aimed a karate chop at an attacking Putty.

Two Putties rushed Kimberly. She backflipped out of reach and landed her combat boots on the chest of another Putty.

Billy zipped in and around the other Putties. They dove at him, but he was too quick. When he whirled around, he saw them lined up in a row.

"Just the way I want you!" Billy shouted.

He leaped up and kicked the first Putty in the chest. The Putty crashed into the one behind him, who tumbled into the next one, and they all toppled down like dominoes.

Just as quickly as the Putties had appeared, they disappeared.

Kimberly dusted off her jeans. "Good work, Billy. You were morphinominal."

Billy smiled, but he looked worried. "I wonder what the Putties were up to. We'd better contact Zordon."

Billy pressed the button on the communicator on his wrist and spoke into it. "Zordon, come in. I sense Rita is up to something."

"Your senses are correct," Zordon replied. "Come to the Command Center at once!"

Billy and Kimberly pressed the teleporter buttons on their communicators. A second later two balls of sparkling light, one pink and one blue, streaked away and materialized inside the secret Command Center.

Alpha 5 whirled over to greet them. "Aye-yi-yi-yi-yi!" the robot cried. His red lights blinked wildly. "We've got trouble!"

Billy and Kimberly turned to Zordon, whose image spoke from inside a column of wavering green light. "My sensors have picked up a strange disturbance in the ocean," Zordon told them.

Kimberly's eyes widened in alarm. "Oh, no! Zack, Jason, and

Trini are diving down there!"

"We know," said Zordon. "And that is where Rita has sent her newest monster."

Alpha pointed to the viewing globe in the center of the room. Kimberly and Billy hurried over to it for a closer look. They couldn't believe what they saw.

A scaly sea monster thundered up and down the Angel Grove beach. Sharp, brown fins ribbed its pink and seaweed-green body. Its webbed feet left enormous footprints in the sand. Three evil-looking fangs jutted out from its two mouths. But the most terrifying thing of all was the one monstrous fish-eye in the center of its forehead.

"Rita calls this new monster the Goo Fish," Zordon explained.

Billy turned pale with fright. He feared all fish. And now he was staring at the biggest, most deadly fish he had ever seen.

The monster spewed a gooey blue spray from one of its mouths. The poison goo melted the sand and made fish leap out of the water in terror.

"It's destroying the ocean!" Kimberly exclaimed.

"You cannot wait for the others," Zordon instructed. "The Goo Fish is extremely dangerous. It destroys anyone and anything it touches. You two must stop the

Goo Fish before it's too late."

Kimberly nodded. "It's morphin time!"

She and Billy raised their Power Morphers to the sky. Just as Zordon had taught them, they called upon the spirits of the ancient dinosaurs.

"Pterodactyl!" cried Kimberly.

"Triceratops!" cried Billy.

Instantly the two teenagers morphed into—Power Rangers! Dressed in their sleek jumpsuits, the Pink and Blue Rangers disappeared in a flash of light—and reappeared at the beach to battle the Goo Fish.

CHAPTER 4

Kimberly and Billy scanned the deserted beach. Shading her eyes, the Pink Ranger gazed out to sea. The blue water showed no sign of her friends—or the Goo Fish.

"Zack, Jason, and Trini are still scuba diving," Kimberly said.

"I have a feeling someone's going to pop up somewhere," Billy said.

Then suddenly, from out of the calm water, rose the monstrous head of the Goo Fish!

Billy jumped back. "This is most disturbing, Kimberly! It's a *fish!* I can't go near it!"

"Come on, Billy. You can handle it," said Kimberly.

Billy whirled and saw the Putties landing in the sand behind him. "I can handle them!" he shouted.

He and Kimberly sprang into action as the Putty Patrol attacked. The Rangers used gymnastics and karate to defend themselves. They fought so hard that the mindless creatures retreated. But as they did, the Goo Fish lurched up on shore.

Bit by scaly bit, the giant fish moved in on Kimberly. "Hey, slime-ball," shouted the Pink Ranger as she tried a karate kick, then a backflip smash. The Goo Fish came on strong, though. Too strong. Now it cornered Kimberly!

"Billy!" she cried. "Give me a hand!"

Billy tried to overcome his fear and raced to Kimberly's side.

Up in her fortress on the moon, Rita screeched in anger. "How dare those power brats try to stop me! They can't win!" she shouted, as she waved her wicked wand frantically in the air.

"How can I stop them?" she shrieked. Then she whirled around and focused her scary dark eyes on Goldar.

Goldar's snout wrinkled as he thought faster than he ever had before. It was a very bad idea not to answer someone who could turn you into a toad or a rock or a tree.

"I've got it!" Goldar roared. "Cast a spell on Billy so he'll be too scared to fight."

The evil empress cackled with delight. "Oooh, I love it!" She clutched her wand and began to chant an evil spell.

It's Friday—yaay! Tomorrow, Jason, Trini, and Zack are going scuba diving! Billy and Kimberly will picnic at the lake!

Bulk and Skull have big plans, too—a fun day of fishing!

Bulk and Skull's lines get tangled up, and they send each other flying into the lake!

The Putty Patrol moves in to ruin Billy and Kimberly's picnic!

After Billy and Kimberly fight the Putties, Billy decides it's time to contact Zordon.

Zordon tells Billy and Kimberly about the Goo Fish, Rita's latest monster.

Billy and Kimberly head to the beach in search of the Goo Fish—but find more Putties instead!

Meanwhile, Goldar gives Rita an idea: "Cast a spell on Billy so he'll be too scared to fight!"

"Billy, you have to face your fear of fish," instructs Zordon as the other Power Rangers listen.

"I will not let this fear take over!" the Blue Ranger announces as he joins the others to finish off the Goo Fish for good!

Now that Billy's overcome his fear of fish, Alpha gives him a fishing rod!

The next day, Billy shows off his catch of the day—but it's got Bulk hooked by the nose!

"Terror, terror, get in gear. Make Billy's fear sharp like a spear. Fill him with fright when a fish comes in sight."

Lightning bolts burst from Rita's magic staff as it drew in waves of terror from all around the world. The air crackled with electricity. Then the evil spell whizzed down to Earth and hit its target.

Billy stopped in his tracks, so terrified he couldn't take another step. "The fish...the fish," he stammered. "I'm too afraid."

"Billy, I need you," Kimberly shouted, backing away from the Goo Fish.

"I can't help," he cried. "I want

to...." But Billy couldn't even move.

"Fight your fears!" Kimberly said.

Again and again, Billy tried to help. But one look at the Goo Fish set his heart pounding in his chest.

Back in the Command Center, Zordon monitored the action on Earth. Kimberly needed help, fast. "Try raising Zack, Trini, and Jason on the communicators, Alpha."

But the teens didn't answer. They were still underwater.

"Aye-yi-yi-yi-yi!" said Alpha. "This is getting serious."

Meanwhile, on the beach, the Blue Ranger crouched into a ball as the Goo Fish closed in on Kimberly. The Pink Ranger bravely leaped at the monster. Blue goo shot out of its mouths onto her Power Boots and glued her to the ground.

"Ugh! What is it?" Kimberly cried. As the Pink Ranger struggled to escape her gooey prison, the monster whipped out a spear. A deadly spear, with a razor-sharp point.

The Goo Fish hefted the spear. Laughing, it took aim.

At the other end of the beach, Zack, Jason, and Trini finally popped their heads out of the water. Sunlight sparkled on the waves as the three swam back to shore. Sea gulls flew lazily overhead. The friends kicked off their flippers and wet suits and pulled on T-shirts and shorts.

Jason gave Zack a high-five. "That was an awesome dive."

"Totally amazing," Zack agreed.

Trini smiled. "I can't believe how beautiful it is down there."

Beep! Beep! Their communicators sounded, shattering the calm. "What is it, Zordon?" Jason asked.

Zordon's deep voice boomed. "Rita has created a new monster. It's called the Goo Fish and it has Kimberly and Billy trapped at the other end of the beach. You must help them immediately!"

"We're on our way!" said Jason. He turned to his friends. "Come on, guys. It's morphin time!"

They held up their Power Morphers.

"Mastodon!" cried Zack and morphed into the Black Ranger.

"Saber-toothed Tiger!" cried Trini and morphed into the Yellow Ranger.

"Tyrannosaurus!" cried Jason and morphed into the Red Ranger.

An instant later, the three Power Rangers teleported to Billy and Kimberly.

"Hey, tuna-brain," shouted Zack to the Goo Fish.

The scaly monster swiveled its head around. When it saw the three Power Rangers, it roared and stabbed its spear at them. The Rangers ducked. Then they leaped up and gave the monster three powerful punches. The evil fish hardly budged. Jason karate kicked the monster, but he slipped on its slimy skin and fell at its feet.

Aiming straight for the Red Ranger, the Goo Fish raised its deadly spear. Zack dashed forward and swung his mighty arm, knocking the spear from the monster's grasp and breaking it in half.

The Goo Fish grunted in anger. Then, surprisingly, it backed away. And with one last roar, the evil fish dove under the waves.

Kimberly breathed a sigh of relief as her friends helped

unstick her from the goo. But where was Billy?

A few feet away, the Blue Ranger rocked back and forth, his knees up against his chest, his teeth chattering in fear. Gently, Kimberly helped him to his feet.

"Quickly," Kimberly told the others. "We'd better get back to the Command Center. Something's really wrong with Billy."

A split second later, the five teens stood before Zordon. "We really had our hands full with that Goo Fish," Jason told Zordon.

"Man," said Zack, "it didn't even feel our punches!"

Billy felt terrible. Now that he was far away from the fish, he wasn't so frightened anymore. But why hadn't he been able to fight it? Why had he been so scared?

"It's all my fault," he said sadly. "I didn't do a thing."

Trini touched his arm. "Don't blame yourself, Billy. Everyone's afraid of something."

"Is there anything we can do to help Billy?" Kimberly asked Zordon.

Jason stepped forward. "We're really going to need him."

"Yeah," said Zack. "That Goo monster is one slippery fish. Everyone has to fight together!"

Zordon nodded. "There is an explanation for Billy's behavior. Rita cast a spell, making Billy more fearful of fish than he's ever been before."

Zordon paused for a moment, then continued. "Billy, you have to face your fear of fish. You had some bad experiences. But that doesn't mean they will happen again. And if you stand up to your fear, you will overcome it. Rita's spell will be broken."

Billy stepped forward. "But Zordon, this monster is a *fish*. How can I face it?"

"You must," Zordon replied. "Behold the viewing globe."

The Power Rangers turned toward the globe. Everyone gasped as they watched Rita's monster spew poison up and down the oceanfront. The poison covered the water, the sand, everything in sight!

"This monster is going to destroy humans and sea life—everything on Earth—if you don't stop it!" said Zordon.

Kimberly, Jason, Trini, and Zack all gathered around Billy. Trini said, "Come on, Billy. I know you can do it." The others nodded in agreement.

"I'll try not to let you down," said Billy.

Everyone cheered. Once again, it was morphin time!

A crackling glow filled the Command Center. And the Power Rangers were gone.

CHAPTER 6

In a flash, the Power Rangers appeared on the beach in front of the Goo Fish just as the Putty Patrol landed on shore once again.

"Can you face the fish, Billy?" asked Kimberly.

The Blue Ranger squared his

shoulders. "I'm ready. Let's do it!" He leaped into the air and slammed a fist into a Putty. The other Power Rangers joined in. But Billy was a one-man fighting machine. He wanted to make up for being scared.

Overwhelmed, the Putties quickly vanished.

"Morphinominal!" the Blue Ranger shouted. And then suddenly Billy froze. The Goo Fish was heading straight for him. Billy turned pale beneath his helmet.

"Oh, no," he cried. "I'm too afraid to move!"

Jason saw the danger. He had to do something—and fast. Jason raised his Power Sword high.

"I'll take on this shrimp-face!" he cried. Leaping forward, he struck the monster. But the Goo Fish struck back harder, and Jason went flying.

Trini and Zack exchanged worried looks. "We need to fight as a team!" Trini cried. They whipped out their Power Weapons and fired together at the monster. But the Goo Fish jumped back, and now a blue stream of goo sprayed from its mouth.

"Watch out!" Kimberly yelled.

But it was too late! The goo covered the Power Rangers' boots and stuck them to the ground.

"Wow! What is this stuff?" Zack exclaimed, trying to lift his feet. It felt as if a million pieces of bubble gum were glued to his boots.

"I don't know what it is," Trini said, "but it's disgusting."

Jason kept struggling. Then he called out to Billy. "We're stuck! Give us a hand!"

"I'll try, Jason," Billy said shakily. He turned toward the Goo Fish—and shrank back in fear. "I can't go near it!"

Suddenly Kimberly jumped out from behind a rock. "I'll cut this fish down to size." She aimed her Power Bow at the monster. The arrow sliced through the air. A direct hit!

Kimberly ran to Trini, Jason, and Zack. "I'll get you out of this terrible muck!"

"Kim, watch out!" the Yellow Ranger shouted.

The Goo Fish had recovered. Now it flung starfish bombs. Sparks flew as one, two, three bombs struck Kimberly.

The Pink Ranger fell to the ground. And the Goo Fish moved in.

"Kimberly!" cried Jason. "We'll help you!"

But he couldn't help. Neither could Trini or Zack. The goo on their boots kept them locked in place.

The Goo Fish hurled fish bomb after fish bomb. First at Kimberly, then at Jason, Trini, and Zack. The

Power Rangers fell to the ground, weak from the blasts.

"Billy!" Jason groaned. "We need your help!"

Billy backed away, horrified. "I can't!"

"You can!" Kimberly gasped, as another bomb hit her.

Billy knew that if he didn't act, his friends wouldn't make it. He forced himself to his feet, took a deep breath and thought, *Zordon told me if I face my fear, I can break Rita's spell.* Billy raised his head proudly. He could fight the monster. He *would* fight it!

"I will not let this fear take over," he shouted. "The Blue Ranger is back!"

CHAPTER 7

The Blue Ranger flipped in the air, high above the Goo Fish. "Here's a taste of your own medicine," he cried, jumping over the monster again and again.

The monstrous eye of the Goo Fish darted back and forth, unable to follow Billy's lightning-quick flips. It grunted in confused anger and shot a goo stream straight up into the sky. Billy twisted, and the goo hurtled down to the ground—splattering all over the Goo Fish! The monster cried out in surprise. It couldn't move!

"You don't scare me anymore, fish-face!" Billy jumped close and gave the Goo Fish a karate kick.

Then he turned to his friends. "Thanks for your support. I faced my fears and broke the spell." Quickly, Billy freed the other Rangers from the goo.

Jason slapped the Blue Ranger on the back. "All right!" he said. "Now we can finally put this herring bone away!"

Kimberly shot her Power Bow into the sky. Zack hurled his Power Ax. Trini threw her Power Dagger.

The weapons magically joined together. Then Jason threw his Power Sword. It locked in place, creating the mighty Power Gun. The glowing weapon dropped into Jason's hand. And the monster was helpless before it.

From the balcony of her fortress, Rita howled in anger, "I'll stop those power brats! Sword-fish blades and seaweed stew. Now you must face my giant *goo!*"

She raised her magic staff and hurled it through space. The staff struck Earth, piercing its surface. The ground shook and lightning flashed as the staff snaked its way to the Goo Fish.

The monster grew and grew and grew…until it loomed high above the treetops. The giant Goo Fish glared down at the Power Rangers.

"We won't let you destroy our ocean!" Jason shouted. "We need Dinozord Power now!"

The Power Rangers held up their Power Morphers.

"Tyrannosaurus!" "Mastodon!" "Triceratops!" "Saber-toothed Tiger!" "Pterodactyl!"

The ground trembled with the

distant sound of five dinosaur robots awakening.

Tyrannosaurus erupted from a steaming crack in the ground.

Mastodon broke through its cage of ice.

Triceratops charged across the scorching desert.

Saber-toothed Tiger leaped through a twisted jungle.

Pterodactyl erupted from the fires of a volcano.

Side by side they raced like the wind to answer the call.

The Power Rangers leaped into the air—then landed in the cockpits of their Dinozords.

"It's time for you to take a trip—to the bottom of the sea!"

Jason shouted from his cockpit.

Two Zords locked into a third, *Clunk! Clang!* and became legs. Two more Zords locked in, *Clang! Thunk!* and formed arms.

The mighty head rose from its chest. Its helmet swung open and locked into place. Its shield clanged into its chest.

The Zords had become a super robot—the Megazord!—with the Power Rangers working the controls.

"Power up the Zord," Jason ordered from his cockpit.

"Battle mode," said Billy.

"Do it!" shouted Jason.

The mighty Megazord thundered toward the Goo Fish. The

two giants battled. Sparks flew with every hit.

Then the monster roared and shot a stream of goo straight at the Megazord.

"We're stuck to the ground," Jason shouted.

The Goo Fish gave a sinister laugh. Then it advanced.

Billy shouted, "We need more power!"

"Right!" said Jason. "Enough of this overgrown guppy. I call for the Mighty Power Sword!"

High up in the sky, the shining Mighty Power Sword appeared.

Crack! Lightning bolts flew through the air as the sword charged up with super-energy.

Then it sliced toward Earth, right into the Megazord's powerful hand. *Snap!* One swipe of the Power Blade cut through the goo that held the Megazord in place.

Holding the sword high, the Megazord surged ahead. Nothing could stop the Rangers now.

The Megazord raised the Mighty Power Sword and took aim. It hit its target, and the Goo Fish fell with a thump.

Sparks rained down. A blanket of dust covered the monster fish. And then it vanished in a cloud of smoke. The deadly destroyer was defeated.

Rita screeched in anger as she saw the whole thing through her magic telescope. She beat at the pointy cones of her hat.

"There, there, Your Awfulness," said Goldar. "One day—one day soon, we'll destroy those Power Rangers for good!"

For now though, Earth was safe once again. Thanks to the Mighty Morphin Power Rangers.

"Congratulations," Zordon told the Rangers when they teleported back to the Command Center. "By destroying the Goo Fish monster, you have saved Earth's precious oceans.

"And Billy," Zordon added, "I would especially like to congratulate you. You faced your fears and overcame them, breaking Rita's spell. Now you are even stronger than before."

Just then Alpha scuttled over. "This is for you," he said, handing Billy a brightly wrapped present.

Billy opened the box. Inside was a fishing rod!

"Now that you've overcome your fear of fish," Alpha added, "I thought this would be the perfect birthday present."

Billy grinned. "That's very thoughtful, Alpha. But it's not my birthday!"

"Uh-oh!" said Alpha, his lights flashing. "Computer default! Aye-yi-yi-yi-yi!"

CHAPTER 8

At the Angel Grove Youth Center the next day, Zack and Jason worked out on exercise equipment while Trini and Kimberly checked out some scuba-diving gear.

But they all rushed over when Billy came in. He held his brand-new fishing rod and a large white bag. Something was wriggling inside.

"Wow, Billy," said Trini. "You really caught something!"

"Morphinominal!" exclaimed Zack.

"I'm proud of you, Billy," added Kimberly. "You really turned your fear around."

"Maybe you'll come scuba diving with us now," Jason said.

Billy smiled. "I'd like that. I think I might actually enjoy it."

Just then Bulk and Skull came into the youth center. Skull was carrying a white bag, too—just like Billy's.

Kimberly stepped back. "It's

starting to smell really fishy around here!"

She pointed to Bulk.

"Yeah?" he said, puffing out his chest. Then he took his bag and set it down next to Billy's. "That's because I caught the king of the sea!"

"Oh, right." Trini laughed.

Annoyed, Bulk strutted to and fro, trying to build up suspense. "Listen up, seaweed-for-brains. I caught the big one. Something none of you nerds could ever get close to. Show 'em, Skull."

Skull opened the bag. Smiling proudly, he pulled out a huge can of tuna fish!

The five teenagers laughed.

"Did you go fishing in the supermarket?" Zack asked.

Bulk didn't answer. He just pulled Skull over by his jacket and snarled. "I told you to buy the biggest fish, sardine-breath!"

"I did! It was the biggest can I could find. Hey, tuna is the only fish I know. And it's your favorite!"

Bulk pushed him away, disgusted. "Okay," he said to Billy, "let's see what you caught." He grabbed Billy's bag.

Billy raised his hand in warning. "Bulk, I'd be careful if I were you. It's a—"

But Bulk had already thrust his face inside.

"—live lobster," Billy finished.

"Arrggh!" Bulk screamed. He pulled his head out of the bag, with the lobster clamped onto his nose!

Bulk pulled and pulled. But it only made matters worse. The lobster just held on tighter.

Billy and the other Power Rangers laughed as Bulk stumbled toward the door. They'd battled the mighty Goo Fish and won.

Surely Bulk could handle one little lobster!